Big Mama's Baby

Lacy Finn Borgo

Illustrated by
Nancy Cote

BOYDS MILLS PRESS

HONESDALE, PENNSYLVANIA

Boyds Mills Press, Inc.
815 Church Street
Honesdale, Pennsylvania 18431
Printed in China

  Library of Congress Cataloging-in-Publication Data

Borgo, Lacy Finn.
  Big Mama's Baby / Lacy Finn Borgo ; illustrated by Nancy Cote.—1st ed.
     p. cm.
  Summary: Having raised Baby, a bull calf, since just after he was born, Big Mama
has a hard time accepting that he is getting too big for her yard.
  ISBN 978-1-59078-187-6 (hardcover : alk. paper)
  [1. Farm life—Fiction. 2. Bulls—Fiction. 3. Human-animal relationships—Fiction.]
  I. Cote, Nancy, ill. II. Title.

PZ7.B6484525Big 2007
  [E]—dc22
                              2006037936

First edition
The text of this book is set in 15-point Minion.
The illustrations are done in acrylic.

10 9 8 7 6 5 4 3 2 1

For my mama, a big mama to many
—L.F.B.

To the love shared by all mamas and their babies,
whoever they are or wherever they may be
—N.C.

THEY LOOKED ALIKE, BIG MAMA AND BABY.
Hair of salt-and-pepper, eyes of dark desert sand, and a
jolly disposition that surfaced whenever they were together.
The only difference—Big Mama was a grandmother and
Baby was a Black Angus calf. Big Mama raised Baby as her
own. Just after he was born, she bought him at the sale
barn and carried him home in the bed of her Chevy truck.

Home was a small speck of a town between Cross Cut and Cottonwood in the Hill Country of Texas. Big Mama lived in an old house near the old Dunmore Halkins ranch. Dunmore Halkins had a herd of Black Angus cows, did a little farming on the side, and was Big Mama's oldest friend.

Big Mama fed Baby twice a day with a rubber nipple attached to a quart Mason jar full of milk. Big Mama would pull up her red-rusted chair and call, "Hey, Baby! Hey, Big Mama's Baby!" and he would come trotting up, stirring up the dusty ground, ready for his feedin' and lovin'. After sucking every last drop of milk from the Mason jar, he settled his head and soggy mouth restfully in her lap for ear and neck scratchin'.

Down at Collum's Café each morning, Big Mama
drank her coffee and listened to folks' talk of town news.
"See you got yourself a new pet," they said.
"Gonna keep that calf in your yard?" they asked.
"None of your business," Big Mama said.
Dunmore just sipped his coffee.

The hot Texas days gave way to cool Texas nights, so
Big Mama slept on the screened-in porch. Each night she fell
asleep to the crickets chirping and an occasional coyote howl.
One night while Big Mama was sleeping, Baby smashed his
nose up against the screen to smell her salt-and-pepper hair.
Then, at the top of his voice, he called, "Biiiggg Maaamaaa!"

She bolted up and screamed, "You scared the jeepers out
of me!" Neighbors' porch lights flashed. Some folks came out
on their porches to see what all the commotion was about. So
Big Mama let him inside. He snuggled his large cow frame
next to her bed and went to sleep.

The next morning down at the café, the townsfolk were talkin'.
"Heard Baby last night," they said.
"Woke the neighborhood," they said.
"Buy some ear plugs," Big Mama said.
Dunmore sipped his coffee and laughed.

Baby followed Big Mama around her yard as she worked. One corner was fenced off with chicken wire so that Big Mama could grow vegetables without Baby having the temptation to eat them. While she worked in compost and watered that hard, dry Texas ground, Baby stood outside the fence and called her name: "Biiiggg Maaamaaa!" She answered him by throwing bug-eaten watermelons and squash over the fence.

After picking all that was ripe, Big Mama loaded up
Baby with saddlebags full of produce from her garden.
She and Baby walked down to the flea market.

The flea market was located at the only traffic light in town.
There, with Baby at her side, Big Mama sold her produce. She
was surrounded by others who sold Pecos cantaloupes, velvet
Elvis paintings, and deer corn.

They didn't mind Baby. In fact, folks stopped just to get a
look at this tame calf that rolled over so you could scratch his
belly. It was good for business and conversation.

Even though Baby wasn't drinking from a bottle anymore, he still wanted to suck. So each evening when they got home from the flea market, Big Mama would sit in her red-rusted chair and let Baby suck on her thumb.

One day Baby saw the last of the okra ripening and he smelled the last of the watermelons. While Big Mama was gone, he broke through the fence and ate until his belly was bulging. Big Mama came home to a trampled and devoured garden. She was angry with him and scolded him loudly to the ears of the neighbors. The next morning down at the café, the townspeople shared their observations.

"Saw Baby eat up your okra," they said.
"Watched Baby trample your watermelons," they said.
"Why didn't you stop him?" Big Mama asked.
Dunmore sighed and sipped his coffee.

Big Mama hated to admit it, but Baby's half-ton body was getting to be more than she could handle. Oh, Baby meant no harm to Big Mama. He only wanted to show her affection, but just laying his huge, soggy head in her lap was heavy enough. On more than one occasion he accidentally knocked her down during a rubbin' and scratchin' session.

Baby's manure was starting to pile up even though Big Mama used as much as she could in her compost. It was only grass and water, but the neighbors were starting to talk about the smell.

The next morning down at the café, Big Mama and Baby were the topic of conversation yet again.

"That bull is too much for you," they said.

"You should take him to the sale barn," they said.

"I won't sell him," Big Mama said.

Dunmore sipped his coffee and thought.

Big Mama was troubled but didn't know what to do. When she got home from Collum's, she noticed her white wooden slat fence was broken and Baby was missing.

She checked the flea market, but folks said, "No Baby."

She checked the café, but the townspeople said, "Haven't seen him."

So Big Mama climbed into her Chevy and went to Dunmore Halkins's ranch. As she was driving up the dirt road, she saw Baby running and playing in Dunmore's wide-open pasture. Dunmore met her at the fence.

"I'll get him home as soon as I can," Big Mama said.

"Let him stay," Dunmore said.

Big Mama missed Baby but visited him often. Here, Baby had all the grass he could eat and lots of land to explore. He was now the bull to a herd of cows. Still, Baby never forgot who his real family was. Whenever Baby heard the *brummp bump*, *brummp bump* of Big Mama's tires over the cattle guard, he came thundering toward her. She reached out the window and rubbed his head, and in return he would call, "Biiiggg Maaamaaa!"